For Alfie, with love

Gill Books
Hume Avenue
Park West
Dublin 12
www.gillbooks.ie

Gill Books is an imprint of M.H. Gill & Co.

© Peter Donnelly 2019
978 0717 1 84811

Designed by www.grahamthew.com
Printed by L&C Printing, Poland

This book is typeset in Baskerville 32 pt.
The paper used in this book comes from the wood pulp of
managed forests. For every tree felled, at least one tree is
planted, thereby renewing natural resources.

5 4 3 2 1

Peter Donnelly

THE PRESIDENT'S SURPRISE

Gill Books

Today was a very special day. It was the President's birthday and there was going to be a very BIG party.

Now, honeybun. You go for a nice long walk while we get everything ready. And don't forget to be back by five!

The President decided to walk his dogs in the Phoenix Park.

All around Áras an Uachtaráin, the work began.

The President's pigeon flew high up to the rooftop where he hung lots of green, white and orange bunting.

Inside, the President's wife planned where everybody would sit.

'Hmmm, we have two guests called Mary,' she thought.

'I'll place one either side of the President. I'm sure they'll have lots of interesting things to talk about.'

Outside, the butler was busy polishing the front door. Nice and shiny, that's the way he liked things to look. After all, it was the most important front door in Ireland!

Meanwhile, the President stopped off at Farmleigh House for some tea and scones.

Back at the Áras, Mrs Mullins, the housekeeper, dusted the picture frames. There were lots of famous people on the walls.

Maybe her portrait would be up there too someday.

In the kitchen, the two chefs prepared some delicious treats, including a VERY special birthday cake.

Yes, it seemed like everything
was going to plan.

At the Wellington Monument, the President found the perfect spot to practise his yoga. Everybody joined in!

Suddenly, the President's wife noticed
the time. Surely the President should
be home by now?

'Where could he have got to?'
she wondered.

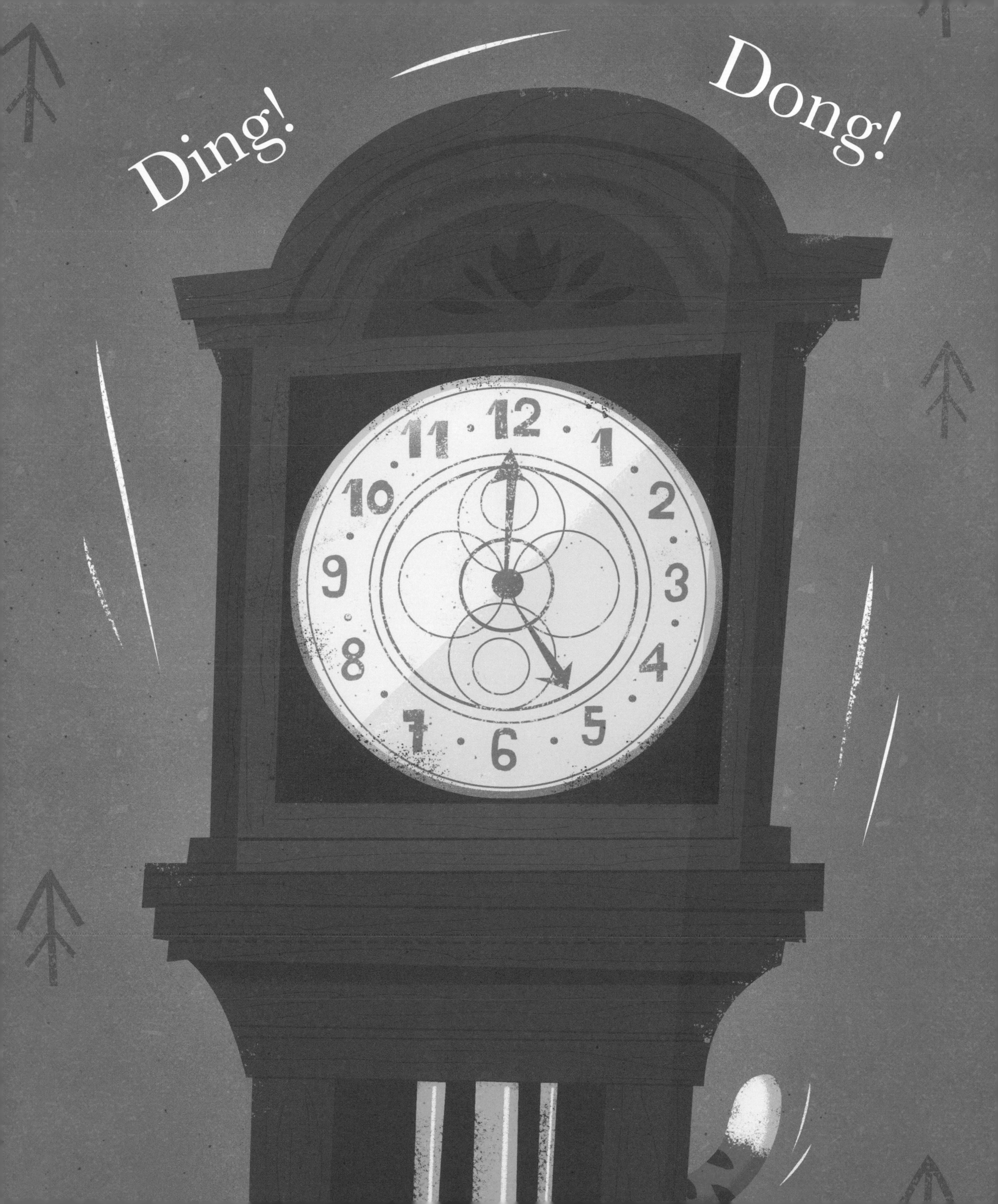
Ding!
Dong!

Áras an Uachtaráin

At the front gates, the guests began to arrive. The President's pigeon counted the line of fancy cars as they entered the Áras.

Click!

Click!

Click!

Click!

There were even presidents from other countries.

Inside, the guests waited for the President.
They waited ...
and waited ...
and waited ...

… but the President was nowhere
to be seen.

Where could he have got to?

'Oh dear!' said the President's wife, 'Could the President have forgotten his own birthday party?'

Everybody looked so disappointed.

When suddenly ...

SURPRISE!

Out of the birthday cake

jumped the **President** himself!

And **what** a surprise it was, too!

The President

There was no need to worry after all.
The President would NEVER forget
his very own birthday party!

He!

He!

He!